Down Under Down Under

Diving Adventures on the Great Barrier Reef

by Ann McGovern

photographs by
Jim and Martin Scheiner and the author

Macmillan Publishing Company   New York

For Dennis Russell Mulligan

ACKNOWLEDGMENTS

Special thanks to Anita and Bruce Bassett of Human Underwater Biology for their kind assistance, to Qantas Airways, to Captain Tony Brigg and the helpful crew of the *Coral Princess*, to Donna McLaughlin and Odile Scheiner for modeling, and once again to Marty Scheiner for his constant encouragement above and below the sea.

Photographs by Martin Scheiner: pages 4, 6, 9, 11, 12, 14, 15 (top right, top left, middle, bottom right), 16, 18 (left, right), 30 (bottom), 34, 38 (top, bottom left, bottom right), 39 (top right, top left, bottom), 40, 41 (top, bottom), 42 (bottom left), 43 (top right, bottom right). Photographs by James B. Scheiner: pages 7, 15 (bottom left), 19 (bottom left, bottom right), 20, 22, 23, 25, 26, 27, 29, 30 (top), 36, 42 (top), 42–43 (bottom), 44, 46. Photographs by Ann McGovern Scheiner: jacket, title page, pages 19 (top), 35 (top, bottom), 43 (top left).

LIBRARY OF CONGRESS CATALOGING-IN-PUBLICATION DATA
McGovern, Ann.   Down under, down under: diving adventures on the Great Barrier Reef/by Ann McGovern; photographs by Jim and Martin Scheiner and the author.—1st ed.   p.   cm. Includes index. Summary: A twelve-year-old girl recounts her experiences on the Great Barrier Reef, encountering sharks, sea snakes, and giant clams, exploring the wreck of a ghost ship, observing shore life, and exploring the reef from a dive boat as well as a helicopter.   ISBN 0-02-765770-1   1. Coral reef fauna—Australia—Great Barrier Reef (Qld.)—Juvenile literature. 2. Scuba diving—Australia—Great Barrier Reef (Qld.)—Juvenile literature. 3. Great Barrier Reef (Qld.)—Juvenile literature. [1. Great Barrier Reef (Qld.) 2. Coral reef animals—Australia—Great Barrier Reef (Qld.) 3. Scuba diving. 4. Underwater exploration.] I. Scheiner, Jim, ill. II. Scheiner, Martin, ill. III. Title.
QL125.M35 1989   508.943—dc19   88-30530 CIP AC

Contents

1

Down Under

I am half bird, half fish as I fly and float, sixty feet below the surface of the sea.

Scuba diving anywhere is always magical for me. But I have to pinch myself underwater to think I am truly diving *down under,* in the warm waters of the Great Barrier Reef of Australia. I am on the other side of the world, below the equator. It's winter at home, but here it's summer. When I was a little girl, I thought that if I dug a hole deep enough I'd reach China. Mom said no, I would get to the waters off Australia.

A few feet away, Mom waves. She is always nearby, thank goodness. On my twelfth birthday, I became a junior certified diver and began diving with Mom every chance I got.

That wasn't too long ago. Even though Mom says I'm a terrific diver, I get nervous about new and unfamiliar waters. And the Great Barrier Reef is the strangest, wildest place!

Starfish grow very large on the Great Barrier Reef.

The corals are huge and colorful. I swim through forests of big sea fans. Some soft corals look like tree branches from a book of fairy tales, in shades of purple, yellow, and red. Some of the hard corals are tipped in bright purple. Some corals look like big boulders; the Australians call them *bommies*.

The fish here are splashed with every color and pattern you can think of, and some are so fantastic you think you are dreaming them up. Some fish are tiny—half the size of a pinky nail. Some, like the sharks, are huge.

Right: Deadly crown-of-thorns starfish

Below: Some soft corals look like fantasy tree branches.

I think about the sharks and shiver, though the water is warm. Mom has me almost convinced that most sharks are not dangerous.

Mom is a cool, calm diver. She has to be. Diving is a big part of her job. She is a marine biologist, and she explores coral reefs all over the world.

Recently her work took her to the Great Barrier Reef. Parts of the Great Barrier Reef are being destroyed by the crown-of-thorns starfish. The starfish eat the little animals whose stony skeletons form the reefs. Mom's research team learned that some years there are many more crown-of-thorns than in other years. It's like an epidemic, but in a few years it cures itself and the number of crown-of-thorns becomes smaller.

Mom says the scientists don't know exactly why this happens. The team thought there might not be another large outbreak for ten years or longer.

Mom was in Australia for two weeks, working in a scientific lab and diving with the other scientists on the reefs. Of course, they couldn't include a twelve-year-old girl.

But when Mom's work was over, she arranged the most terrific Christmas present: a ten-day dive trip on the Great Barrier Reef, living on a boat called the *Coral Princess* and diving every day—sometimes as often as three times a day!

It's odd to actually live on a dive boat, instead of staying at a hotel and going out each day to dive at a different dive site. Mom says that a live-aboard dive boat is the only way to get to some of the faraway reefs.

The *Coral Princess* is a big boat—110 feet. It's really like a floating hotel. There are eighteen divers aboard. They've come from all over the world to dive the Great Barrier Reef.

Our dive boat, the *Coral Princess*

A crew of five takes care of everything. It includes Chris, the captain, Sharon, the dive master, and Sharon's assistant, Dennis. Odile is a great cook. Sometimes she makes shark-shaped cookies, and we joke how more people eat sharks than sharks eat people. Peter knows how to do everything—from driving the boat to repairing underwater cameras.

Mom and I share a roomy cabin, but I have the upper berth and bump my head every time I go to bed.

We eat all our meals on the boat in the dining room. There's even a lounge with shelves of books about the underwater life on the Great Barrier Reef.

Mom has promised ten days of diving. And already I've had the most thrilling experience of my life.

2

The Monsters at Cod Hole

Nobody will ever believe me when I tell them what I dived with today at Cod Hole. The huge, white monster fish with large, black spots looked like something out of a horror movie. Potato cods are what they're called in Australia, but I've never heard of a 200-pound potato! Mom says the potato cod is really an unusual species of white grouper.

As soon as I got over the shock of seeing these blimps underwater, I began to count. I must have counted ten of them.

At first, six potato cods swam around Sharon, our dive master. She held a bucket of bait fish and sat on a large coral head. Four or five of the giant fish pushed one another out of the way to get nearer to Sharon's food. Brave Sharon. She fed them by hand.

She petted them and patted them and even scratched one under its huge chin. I could hardly believe my eyes when I saw that big fish roll over on its side, begging for more food. A circus below the sea!

Then, when they had their fill of the bait fish, they began cruising among the rest of us. Soon I was touching them as they swam around me on the reef. What a thrilling feeling!

What I loved the best is that these huge creatures could be so gentle and tame, almost like puppy dogs following me around. Two-hundred-pound puppies!

Back on the boat, Captain Chris said, "Did you notice how the potato cods slurped in their food? Kind of like a vacuum cleaner."

Suddenly I wondered about their eyesight. What if the potato cods have poor vision, like those other big fish, the sharks? What if they thought my arm was a new kind of food? Would they slurp in my arm like a vacuum cleaner?

Feeding the giant potato cod

A 200-pound monster

I can't figure out Captain Chris. A captain of a live-aboard dive boat should be serious. But he's a big tease. The problem is I don't know when he's teasing and when he's being serious.

The first day on board he seemed surprised that a twelve-year-old girl was on a Great Barrier Reef dive trip.

"Why, even old experienced divers find these reefs a mighty challenge," he said. "Especially with the shark feeding and the deadly sea snakes we'll encounter."

Deadly sea snakes? Sharks?

And I thought nothing could be more thrilling than diving with the fat potato cods of Cod Hole. Little did I know.

3

About the Great Barrier Reef

When I told my friends I was going to the Great Barrier Reef, they wanted to know why it was so special.

First of all, it's huge! Picture a coral reef that stretches underwater from New York to Florida! The Great Barrier Reef is 1,250 miles long, extending from northeastern Australia to the shores of Papua New Guinea.

It's not one long reef, though. It's made up of 2,000 scattered reefs plus small, tree-covered islands and low, sandy islands called *cays,* separated by winding channels.

Just think! The Great Barrier Reef is the world's largest living thing. Yet it was built by individual pea-sized animals called *polyps.* The polyps' limestone skeletons piled on top of each other over the centuries, building huge reefs, each different than the others.

At low tide, I see the top of the reef breaking the surface of the water. Captain Chris says that there are about 1,500 species of fish living on the Great Barrier Reef and 400 different kinds of coral.

Left: An underwater coral table

This page: So many butterfly fish!

I was going to keep a list of the fish and coral I see, but with so many varieties it would turn out to be an encyclopedia!

The Great Barrier Reef must look the same today as it did in 1770, when British explorer Captain James Cook ran his ship aground on a coral reef. Captain Cook then spent four months charting what he called "submerged rock piles." Chris says it was a pity there were no face masks or snorkels or fins in those days. If Captain Cook had seen the unbelievable corals that he called "rock piles," he would have been just as amazed as I was.

The corals are absolutely awesome. And the colorful fish are out of a dream, too. I think about one family of fish—the butterfly fish. The masked butterfly, the long-snouted butterfly, the beaked butterfly, the banner butterfly—Chris says he can fill half a page with all the different names of this one family of fish.

Chris says that the Great Barrier Reef can be seen from the moon! Maybe one day I'll be able to walk on the moon, look down, and see the Great Barrier Reef. But right now, I'm thrilled to be on a boat on the Great Barrier Reef, looking up at the moon.

Long-snouted butterfly fish

4

Odd Creatures

Every dive is like a wild dream come true. In my journal I write about some of the weird creatures I saw on *one* dive alone—

- funny-faced clown fish that live in a very strange home
- a school of one-horned unicorn fish
- a lumpy, frilly wobbegong shark
- five different, beautifully colored snails without shells, and a big one that I named ET.

After the dive and showers and a big lunch, Mom and I go into the lounge and begin tackling the books. I learn lots of fascinating facts about what I've seen on the morning dive.

A family of clown fish lives in each large anemone. They seldom swim more than a few feet away from their home. The clown fish are the only creatures that are safe from the stinging cells of the anemone's tentacles.

The anemone clearly protects the little clown fish. But what does the anemone get from the clown fish? Mom says that the colorful clown fish attract other fish to the anemone. These fish

Left: A clown fish in its anemone home.   *Right:* The strange unicorn fish.

are stung by the anemone's writhing mass of tentacles and become the anemone's dinner.

Whenever I get too close to the clown fish, they quickly dive down into the anemone's tentacles. I could watch the darling clown fish for hours.

I love unicorns, even though I know they're not real. But unicorn fish are real. Today I saw a school of them—about twenty unicorn fish. Each one had a large spike that stuck out of its head, like the single horn of a unicorn.

Another weird creature is the wobbegong, or carpet shark. The one we saw was bigger than Mom. It's a harmless shark if it's left alone by divers. Sharon spotted it. If I hadn't been looking carefully, I wouldn't have known it was there. Colored brown and gray, it's hard to see on the brownish gray reef it lives on. The weedy growth around its mouth looks like whiskers and

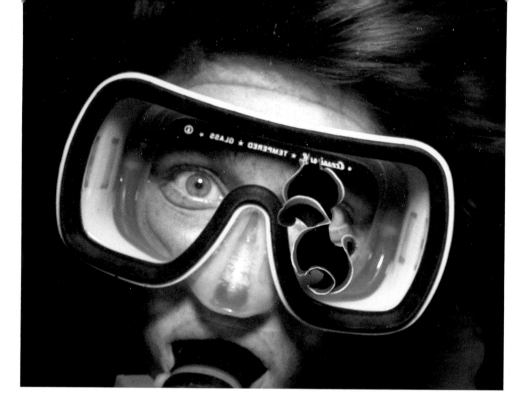

Above: A flatworm floats by my mask. *Below:* Colorful nudibranchs

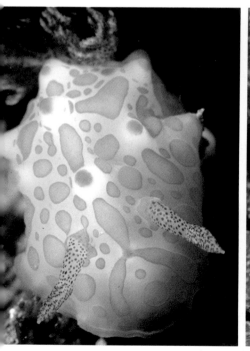

helps to hide its mouth. Sharon says the wobbegong is found only in Australia.

The underwater photographers are delighted with the beautiful snails without shells, molluscs called *nudibranchs*. Nudibranch means "naked gill," and I could see their gills on their backs, looking like delicate plumes. There are dozens of species of nudibranchs on the Great Barrier Reef, most of them no bigger than two inches. But the one I found and named ET was the biggest nudibranch the crew had ever seen. Even Sharon, who knows all these creatures so well, had never seen anything like it before.

I measured ET—nearly a foot long!—and then we put it into a bucket to study. We'll return it to its watery home this afternoon.

I feel like a scientist making an important discovery.

ET—the big nudibranch!

5

Sea Snakes

I can't sleep. Over and over I hear the excited talk of the divers.

The sea snakes are poisonous.

Deadly. Venomous.

One bite and you've had it.

Cousin to the cobra. Ten times more deadly.

I toss and turn while the *Coral Princess* heads out to the reef where the sea snakes await.

It's morning. I'm usually the first one in the water. But not today. Mom says I can skip the sea snake dive if I want to. But everyone else is going in, even Chris, who for once doesn't tease me. He looks serious, which makes me even more nervous.

But I'm so curious. I want to see those sea snakes!

Finally I get in the water. I look down and gasp. Seven snakes are slithering through the sea—right toward me. There are snakes to the right of me, snakes to the left of me, snakes everywhere. This place is a snake pit!

A sea snake gets curious about a fin.

I look at Chris. Is he crazy? He's holding a writhing snake in his gloved hand so one of the underwater photographers can take its picture. One twist of the snake's head and Chris could be bitten.

Now other divers are picking up the paddle-tail snakes. Some of them are four feet long!

I'm making this dive because I'm curious, but it seems the sea snakes are even more curious. One is slithering around my fin.

Enough is enough. I head for the surface—and so does the snake, who hasn't finished investigating every bit of my fin.

Finally I reach the ladder and get safely on the boat. Mom is right behind me.

"You're a brave girl," she says, "but you really have nothing to fear."

Has too much diving affected my dear mom's brain? The sea snakes are ten times more deadly than the cobra and I have nothing to fear?

"A sea snake has tiny fangs all the way back in its upper jaw," Mom explains. "It's very hard for a snake to bite us, and really, no snake wants to eat us. We don't taste as good as fish. Unless we handle a snake too roughly, it's no danger to us."

Mom looks at my doubtful face. "Honest and truly," she says.

So on the second dive, who is that diver holding a sea snake for the photographers? Me, that's who.

The captain holds a venomous sea snake.

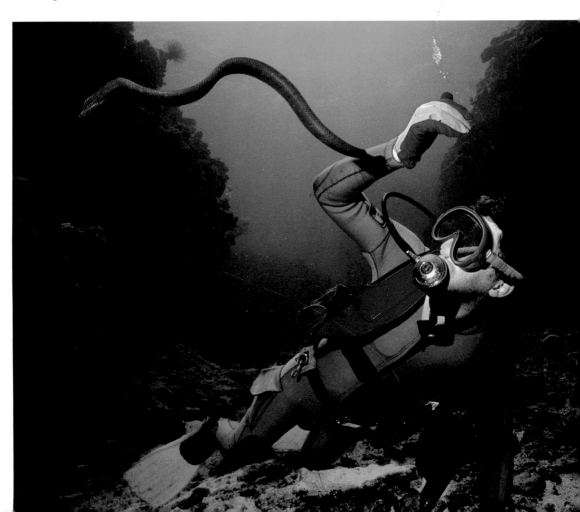

6

Shark Feeding

"Okay, Miss Brave Diver," Chris greets me one bright, sparkling, warm morning. "Are you ready for your next thrill?"

I shake my head no. I am still getting over the excitement of diving with sea snakes.

Chris grins. "Our next dive is Shark Reef, where there are lots of sharks. We're going to feed the sharks," he says. I notice he doesn't say feed *me* to the sharks.

"By hand." Chris's grin gets bigger.

"Not my hand," I say. "No way."

Sharon comes to my rescue. "What we'll do is throw in bits of fish, the kind of food that gray reef sharks love, and soon . . ."

"Soon you'll be surrounded by sharks. Big sharks," Chris says.

Sharon looks at my face and quickly says, "You won't be in the water. We'll be watching the sharks from the platform."

At lunch, the divers swap shark tales. Lunch is spaghetti, my favorite, but I can't eat it. Sharon whispers, "Don't believe everything you hear."

The gray reef shark, a magnificent animal

The divers gather at the platform. The chain holding the platform has been loosened a little so that the end of the platform is a couple of inches underwater.

I am given the safest place, wedged in between Mom and Marty, the biggest diver on the boat. Even a shark might be scared off by Marty.

We lie on our tummies with our face masks on. My head is over the edge of the platform—right in the water.

Right away I count six sharks swimming below us. I feel surrounded by sharks, but they are circling slowly and lazily and I admire their grace.

Then Chris throws in fish scraps and everything changes—fast. The sea begins to move and heave. I see white foam and waves on the water. Only a minute before the sea was as smooth as silk.

Through my face mask I see a big six-foot gray reef shark rush to the fish, open its jaws wide, and swallow it down. Then another

Coming in for food

big shark zooms up. The six sharks devour every scrap of fish Chris throws them. They go into a frenzy and bump each other blindly. Now two more have joined them.

One shark heads for our platform. Its body is on the sloping end of the platform! The platform is shaking! Mom tightens her grip on me. Just when I think it might be my last moment on earth, the shark bolts away.

Chris has put a rope through a big piece of fish. A shark bites on it, and Chris hauls the shark out of the water. There is no fish hook! That shark just won't let go of its food. Chris drops the shark back into the water.

Chris has stopped feeding the sharks. Now they calm down and circle the boat. I feel safe again. I look at their streamlined bodies. How majestic they are! I think of the movies about sharks that scared me so, though I know that most sharks are harmless.

But later I find out that the gray reef sharks are counted among the handful of dangerous sharks.

Mom says they're slower than most other sharks. "Most fish move so quickly that they are able to take cover before a gray reef attacks," she says. "Gray reef sharks seek slower, weak fish—not people. To them, we're probably just things that might steal their food. So the sharks will put on a show to drive us away. They'll shake their heads wildly. If we keep our distance, so will the grays."

"Don't worry, Mom," I say. "The view of their teeth today is the closest I ever want to have."

Will anyone back home believe me when I tell them I was just inches away from dangerous gray reef sharks?

A shark comes too close.

7

The Wreck of the Ghost Ship

One morning I awake to high seas and a strong wind. Will we have to cancel our plans to dive the wreck of the ghost ship *Yongala*? Chris is walking around with an expression of gloom and doom.

"The *Yongala* is all great dives rolled into one," he says. "I'd hate for you to miss it."

Should I believe Captain Chris's talk of fish the size of Volkswagons, millions of schooling fish, sea snakes, and always a tough current to swim against?

Do I really want to make this dive? The story of the *Yongala* gives me goose bumps. She was a 350-foot steamship, modern in every way. In March 1911, she disappeared mysteriously with 121 passengers and a cargo that included a famous racehorse. There was never any trace of the passengers or crew. But days later, the horse was found, washed ashore, its body half-eaten by sharks.

In the years that followed, fishermen reported seeing a ghostly steamer that fitted the *Yongala*'s description—in the very same waters where she had vanished!

Thirty-four years later, in 1945, the wreck of the ship was discovered by a mine sweeper on patrol.

Floating over the ghost ship *Yongala*

Above: A huge turtle swims by.   *Below:* The wreck is covered with soft coral.

"Only in the past few years have divers explored the *Yongala*," Chris tells me. "You need special equipment to find her, like sidescan sonar. There are no markers in the open seas under which she lies."

The wind is howling. I think about the strong currents, the shark-eaten horse, the sea snakes. Is one shipwreck worth the risks?

We reach the site after lunch. The wind is still blowing. Everyone—except me—is eager to make the dive. Mom says I shouldn't dive if I feel nervous.

Chris makes up his mind. "Let's go for it," he says. "But stay close to your dive buddy."

I make up my mind, too. How many times in my life can I see fish the size of a small car?

First some of the crew, slightly seasick, go down to attach heavy lines to the wreck. Four divers jump in and go hand over hand down the line. Mom and I follow, pulling ourselves down the line against the strong current. The visibility is awful. I can see only about twenty-five feet in front of me. Now I see a school of big batfish, then a school of huge barracuda. And there, in front of me, is the shadowy wreck, lying on its side.

I'm right over the keel of the *Yongala*. The wreck is completely covered with hard and soft corals. Masses of tropical fish swim in and out of the corals.

Another diver passes me in this soupy fog. I see a very large sea snake swimming away from us, thank goodness. Mom and I swim forward. In the limited visibility, everything looks shadowy, like a dream. Big jacks, tuna, and other streamlined ocean fish cut through thick clouds of millions of finger-sized bait fish.

We reach the bow of the *Yongala*. It's very dark. What is lurking in the shadows? I stay very close to Mom. Then I see huge rays, one above the other, the currents rippling through their great, winglike bodies. On the sand is a giant sea bass, weighing about 500 pounds. It must be nearly three times the size of a potato cod. As big as a Volkswagon? Well, almost. There are fish everywhere. I look over my shoulder to see a huge turtle swimming by.

We swim under the bridge. The deck is covered with tons of oysters. Could this be where the doomed passengers sat on their deck chairs enjoying the tropical evening?

Though I feel I've only been diving on the *Yongala* a few minutes, our time is up.

Suddenly I am aware of a steady throbbing. For a moment I have the crazy idea that it is the *Yongala*'s engines! But of course it can't be. It's only the anchor of the *Coral Princess* banging against a beam.

Stately batfish and twenty barracuda keep us company on the way up. This dive has been like a dream. I am mesmerized by the teeming concentration of so much life in one place and by the mysterious tale of a mighty ship.

Chris is right. It has been the best dive of my life. But then, everything about the Great Barrier Reef is sensational.

8

Worries on the Reef

"Have you ever seen a clam as big as a pony?" Chris asks at lunch. Is our captain teasing me again?

"Well, you've got a treat in store today," he says. "You'll be exploring our giant clam gardens. And you won't need your scuba gear. You can snorkel over them since they're in shallow water.

"But be careful," Chris warns. "The old sea stories are filled with tales of sailors getting trapped in giant clams when they snapped shut. There are about 500 of these Tridacna clams in our clam garden."

I wonder if Chris is up to his old teasing tricks. But I remember seeing a drawing of a human arm caught helplessly in a giant clam in an old book of Mom's.

I'm only a little girl, I think. I'll never get myself free if I get caught in a clam.

I look at Mom, who winks at me. That Chris! I'll never believe him again.

I have trouble believing those giant clams are real. Their mantles range in color from bright blue to emerald green to chocolate brown. When I swim over them, they do close—but gently.

Later Chris says he is glad I didn't dig one up. How could I? The big ones weigh more than 200 pounds!

Chris says that the clams are protected by law. Nobody is allowed to collect any. It used to be that people gathered them for food and for their shells. They used them for decoration, or even as footbaths! They were becoming very rare—almost extinct.

Mom gets so mad at people who don't think before they collect anything from the sea. Shell collectors kill a live animal when they take a shell from the water. And people who take a sea fan or a lovely coral from a reef kill something living, too.

Probably this clam is at least one hundred years old.

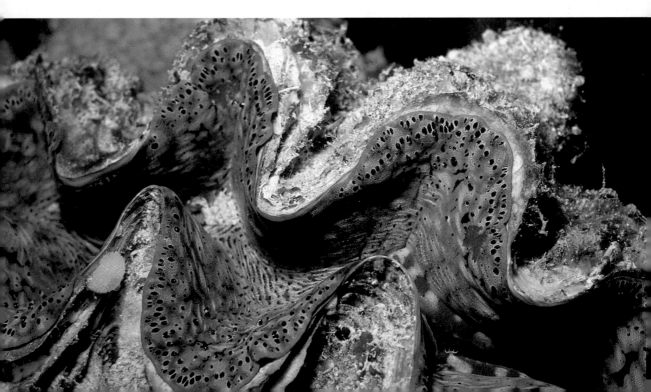

Above: A delicate feather star on soft coral

Below: Another on purple-tipped hard coral

I take something from the reef every time I dive. I take a lifetime of memories. I'll never forget the starfish, red and brown and yellow and blue. Or the coral walls covered with orange and yellow sea fans. And clinging to the sea fans, delicate feather stars—red and black or edged in silver—unbelievable!

There's nothing in the world like these treasures of the reef.

That's why Mom and I get mad at people who rob the reef. It's bad enough that the coral reef has a natural enemy—the crown-of-thorns starfish which Mom has been studying.

Mom says that a certain large mollusc called the triton trumpet is the only creature that hunts and devours the destructive crown-of-thorns. And since shell collectors take the triton trumpet out of the sea, more coral is in danger of being killed by the crown-of-thorns.

This may look like a weed, but it's a fish, a cousin to the sea horse!

9

Memories

The trip is over. The days flew by so quickly. I'm so glad I wrote in my journal every day. Right now all my dives are jumbled together in my mind. The brilliantly colored fish are tumbling around my brain like colored jelly beans.

I think of the juvenile emperor angelfish, its body covered with bright blue and green swirls and curls. I remember how totally different the adult emperor angel looked, with blue and yellow horizontal stripes.

And I remember the night dive we made and the sleeping fish I could pick up in my hand. One red lionfish swam slowly in the darkened overhang of the reef. That's one fish I'd never pick up! Its tips are filled with poison to sting its prey.

Luckily I didn't meet up with a blue-ringed octopus. One bite and you're dead in five minutes.

One day I was poking along a reef when suddenly I felt someone give me a hard push. It was Sharon, warning me away from a reef where a deadly scorpion fish sat. The creature was disguised so well that it was almost impossible to see. Its spines are full of venom, too.

Beautiful starfish

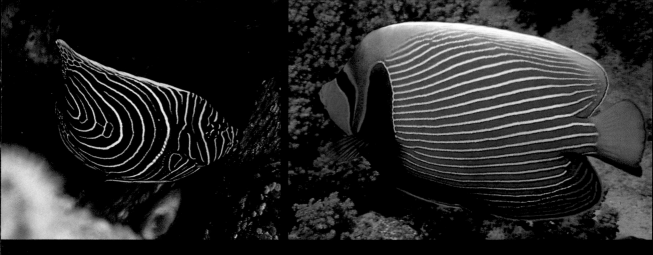

Above left: Juvenile emperor angelfish. *Above right:* The adult emperor looks very different. *Below:* A sleeping lionfish.

Oh, the adventures I've had! One thrilling evening we anchored near a sandy island. It was the time of the year when loggerhead, hawksbill, and green turtles crawl ashore to lay their eggs. We took our outboard to the island after dark.

I was the first to see turtle tracks! The tracks led to where one 300-pounder was digging a pit on the beach. It took her about an hour to fill up the hole with one hundred eggs the size of Ping-Pong balls, hissing sighs and oozing tears with the effort.

When she had finished, I followed her down to the sea. I watched her from the beach until she swam out of sight. I felt terribly sad. Neither she nor I would see her hatchlings. Two months from now, one hundred newly hatched turtles will dig themselves out and crawl to the sea, most falling victim to birds and fish.

I spot the turtle's tracks.

Above: She digs a pit for her eggs. *Below:* She crawls back to the sea.

Watching that turtle lay her eggs had to be the best experience of my life. But so was the wreck of the *Yongala*. And the sea snakes and the shark feeding. Just diving the Great Barrier Reef every day was like falling into a giant aquarium.

Left: Striped toby puffer

Below left: A hawkfish sits on its coral perch.

Below right: Fire gobies dart backward into the sand when we get too close.

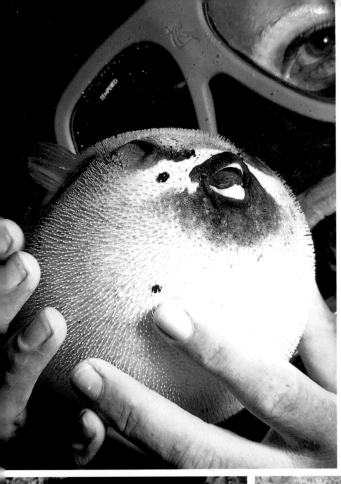

Left: I hold a pufferfish.

Right: Harlequin tuskfish

Lower right: A rainbow of
Christmas-tree plume worms

Even from the air, as we fly home, the reef looks unreal, like a shining green and blue painting. My memories will stay with me forever.

The coral reef from the air

Getting Ready for a Dive

Having the right diving equipment is so important, Mom says. And Sharon adds that it's crucial to know how to use the equipment, too. I learned how in my scuba diving course.

I wear a wet suit made of a kind of rubber called neoprene foam. Some divers wear T-shirts and jeans. The waters of the Great Barrier Reef are nice and warm, about seventy-eight degrees. But when you've been under for a while, your body gets cold. Also, a wet suit is good protection against stinging or scratching coral you accidentally bump into.

With my fins on my feet, I move through the water easily and don't have to swim using my arms.

My face mask helps me see clearly underwater.

My weight belt has just the right amount of weight on it to help me get down without swimming hard.

My *buoyancy compensator,* or BC, is like a vest. I put a little air into the BC so that I stay underwater without sinking or rising. If I put more air into the BC, I'll float up.

All suited up and ready for a dive

The most important piece of equipment is my tank of compressed air. It weighs about thirty pounds on land, but it's weightless in the water.

My regulator attaches to the valve on the air tank. The other part of my regulator goes in my mouth. I breathe in, nice and easy, as long as there is air in the tank. And in order to know just how much air I do have in the tank, I look at my pressure gauge.

My dive watch shows how long I've been diving, and my depth gauge shows how deep I go.

Dive gloves help if I have to hold onto coral. There are stinging cells in lots of coral. I try never to touch any coral so I won't damage it.

A dive light is a must for all night dives. But it's good to take along on day dives, too. I can shine my light underneath an overhang and see the creatures who hide there during the day.

It takes me about fifteen minutes to get into my dive gear. And then *splash!* I'm in the water, into my kind of heaven!

Index